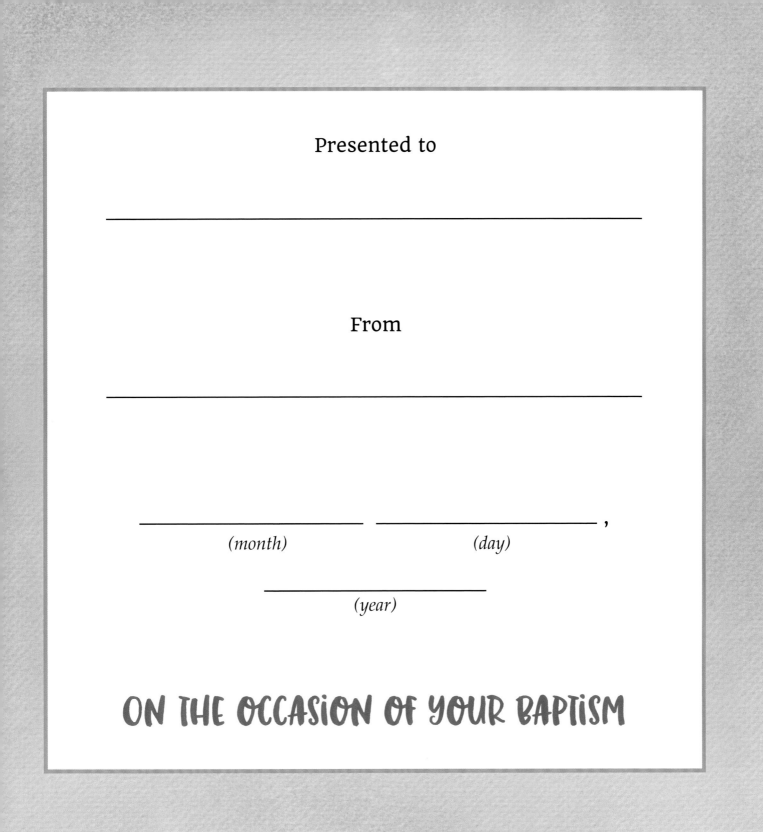

Presented to

_____

From

_____

_____ _____ ,
(month)   (day)

_____
(year)

ON THE OCCASION OF YOUR BAPTISM

25 24 23 22 21 20 19   1 2 3 4 5 6 7 8

ISBN: 978-1-5064-5552-5

Cover design by Mighty Media

Library of Congress Cataloging-in-Publication Data

Names: Young, Taylor, author. | Schmidt, Anita (Illustrator), illustrator.
Title: On the Day You Were Baptized / written by Taylor Young;
illustrated by Anita Schmidt.
Description: First edition. | Minneapolis, MN : Beaming Books, 2019. |
Summary: Relates, through illustrations and easy-to-read text, events of
the joyous day when an infant was baptised, splashed with water and
immersed in the love of family, friends, and God.
Identifiers: LCCN 2018043191 | ISBN 9781506455525 (hard cover : alk. paper)
Subjects: | CYAC: Baptism--Fiction. | Christian life--Fiction. |
Love--Fiction.
Classification: LCC PZ7.1.D493 On 2019 | DDC [E]--dc23
LC record available at https://lccn.loc.gov/2018043191

Beaming Books
510 Marquette Avenue
Minneapolis, MN 55402
Beamingbooks.com

ON THE DAY YOU WERE BAPTIZED

BY TAYLOR YOUNG

ILLUSTRATED BY ANITA SCHMIDT

beaming books

MINNEAPOLIS

On the day you were baptized,
the heavens rejoiced.
We rejoiced too.
It was a very happy day.

That morning, we dressed you in special clothes and wrapped you in a special blanket.

We gazed into your eyes and smiled.
It was your day.

We took you to church,
where everyone was gathered—

our family, our friends,
a whole crowd of people who loved you.

God was there too,
loving you and welcoming you,
just like everyone else.

When the time came,
we brought you to the front
where a bowl of water sat waiting.

We spoke special words.
We promised to love you and care for you always.
We promised to teach you about God's love
and be good role models for you.

Then the water came down,
dribbling, splashing
over your forehead,
covering you
like God's love,
and our love too.

"Welcome, child of God," our church family said.
"You are loved."

You were just a little baby,
and you probably won't remember that special day.

But you can still feel the water on your forehead
when you're in the bath,

or diving deep in the swimming pool,

or walking
through the rain,

and know that
you're still covered
with the love that
was showered on you,

on the day you were baptized.

MEMORIES

MEMORIES

_____

_____

_____

_____

_____

_____

_____

_____

_____

_____

_____

_____

_____

_____

_____

_____

_____

_____

_____

_____

_____

_____

_____

_____